SON OF MINOS

TRINITY PRIMARY ACADEMY
Bounds Green Road
Wood Green
N22 8ES
020 8888 3736
Email: admin@trinityprimaryacademy.org

SON OF MINOS

Samir Bougrine

Copyright © 2016 by Samir Bougrine.

Library of Congress Control Number:		2016902192
ISBN:	Hardcover	978-1-5144-6482-3
	Softcover	978-1-5144-6481-6
	eBook	978-1-5144-6480-9

All rights reserved. No part of this book may be reproduced or transmitted in any form or by any means, electronic or mechanical, including photocopying, recording, or by any information storage and retrieval system, without permission in writing from the copyright owner.

This is a work of fiction. Names, characters, places and incidents either are the product of the author's imagination or are used fictitiously, and any resemblance to any actual persons, living or dead, events, or locales is entirely coincidental.

Any people depicted in stock imagery provided by Thinkstock are models, and such images are being used for illustrative purposes only.
Certain stock imagery © Thinkstock.

Print information available on the last page.

Rev. date: 02/08/2016

To order additional copies of this book, contact:
Xlibris
800-056-3182
www.Xlibrispublishing.co.uk
Orders@Xlibrispublishing.co.uk

CONTENTS

Chapter 1   Jack and Lily Stone 1

Chapter 2   Oops, I Didn't Think of That 8

Chapter 3   Say Hello to Leon 11

Chapter 4   Camp Nikas 15

Chapter 5   A Cursed Blade 21

Chapter 6   The Son of Minos 27

Chapter 7   The Minotaur 31

Chapter 8   It's Just Another Message Written in Blood 39

Chapter 9   Cool! A Chocolate Milk Dispenser 44

Chapter 10   Uninvited Guests 51

Chapter 11   A Mother's Intuition 57

Chapter 12   Crete 62

Chapter 13   Lily Knocks Out a Famous,
             Extremely Muscular Greek Bandit 67

Chapter 14   The Labyrinth 71

Chapter 15   Into Tartarus 75

Chapter 16   Back Home 79

CHAPTER 1

Jack and Lily Stone

Sat next to his younger sister, Lily, Jack was breathing in the sulphurous air around him. He had always hated sleeping in the Sterlings' attic. But unfortunately, Alistair and Mary Sterling were (excluding Ed) their only family left. He was also waiting for a call—a yell, actually—from his idiot of a cousin, Edward Sterling. Ed was ruthless, horrible, and rather unpleasant. He was also the only child Jack's aunt and uncle had. He had recently joined a gang, and despite being the youngest member, he was the most powerful and most feared. He'd always hated Jack and Lily ever since they had arrived in the Sterlings' small yet extremely posh apartment. And so did Jack and Lily's aunt and uncle. Mary and Alistair hated the Stones; Jack and Lily despised them.

Jack had been sent here after two years in care, aged five. It was due to the unfortunate event of his mother and father's, Daniel and Tamara Stone's, death. Jack had loved his parents, but he had never been told how they had died. Whenever he brought up the subject, his aunt and uncle would simply ignore him. But Jack knew they knew something.

Jack was thirteen and loved sport. He played for his school football team as a centre forward. Ever since he was little, he had supported Chelsea, and according to his aunt and uncle, his father had once *played* for the team.

Whenever Jack had a football match, he would always walk to wherever the match took place with his sister. Lily was the only person who ever came to watch Jack play. The others didn't really care, but Jack didn't mind.

Once during a match day, Jack had grown tired of walking and had once tried taking the Sterlings' car. After finding out, they had bruised him and had even threatened to kill him as well. They weren't very benevolent people.

'Jack?' Lily looked up from her phone, a very rare thing. 'Are you okay?'

'Um. . . yeah, yeah. I'm fine.'

Lily could tell something was wrong with her brother, Jack. She stared at his long spiky blond hair that he had inherited from their mum. She had got her dad's brown hair, but she didn't mind. Her brother's eyes were still the same bluish colour they had always been, and as usual, they seemed as if they were thinking about a painful subject. She stared back at her phone screen. She was texting her best friend, Mo. She couldn't wait for the sleepover she had planned for them. Mo had always been her best friend ever since she had started reception school at Beachwood Primary. Lily and Mo were always together. No one could separate them. Lily's friends had joked that not even a chainsaw could do the job. Once, when Lily was in Year 5, Mrs Brown had sent her out for talking and constantly drawing pictures in her maths book. Just for her, Mo had got himself in trouble so he could sit outside and talk to her. They really were stuck like glue. But once Mrs Brown had heard laughter, they knew that they were dead meat.

Meanwhile, Lily typed random letters and numbers rapidly on her phone. Jack couldn't believe he hadn't been called down yet. He was about to calm down and relax, when suddenly. . .

'*Stone!*' Ed scolded. 'Get down here. . . *now!*'

Jack trudged down the stairs. He had promised himself that one day, when he had the chance, he would hack Ed to pieces. Life with the Sterlings was getting extremely irritating and annoying.

'What is it now, Ed?' Jack asked, knowing he wasn't going to like the answer.

'You forgot to give me my three eggs—you only gave me one—and where exactly are my sausages?'

Jack stood there receiving what seemed to feel like a one-hour lecture on how to serve eggs correctly and to never forget that a sausage a day keeps the doctor away. Jack was pretty sure that it was supposed to be an apple, but to be a hundred per cent honest, he didn't really care at all. He would let this fat pig eat all he wanted, and one day, unexpectedly, he would poison him. Well, at least that was what he had had planned for the boy.

Suddenly, Jack felt anger boiling inside him. He didn't realise it at first, but ominously, his hand was automatically forming a fist. Jack felt rage running through his bones. But what was it? Was it anger? Irritation? And most importantly, could this finally be the moment that Jack would hack Ed to tiny pieces? Could it?

Angrily, Jack's veins began to bulge. He began to sweat, and he knew this was it. This was the time when he would get his revenge. He wasn't going to let him get away with being rude to him any more. He wasn't a slave.

Suddenly, Ed noticed Jack's fist turning into some sort of violent purple-coloured plum. He began to laugh. Ed was part of a gang. This skinny little boy probably couldn't even punch properly.

But something Ed didn't know—Jack had the element of surprise on his side. Ed never paid attention to Jack, and therefore, he had no idea that Jack and Lily went to karate classes, both of them black belts.

Ed brushed a large lump of dark brown hair out of his round face. 'Go on then. Try something.'

Ed stretched his arms out like the Brazilian statue Christ the Redeemer.

Even though he had always hated Ed and had promised himself one day he would finish him off, Jack didn't want to hurt his cousin. His martial arts teacher had only told him to fight if absolutely necessary and to never throw the first punch. He waited. Ed didn't move. Neither did Jack. They spent that moment in complete silence. Until . . .

'Before we start fighting,'—Jack didn't like where this was going—'if you're gonna go cry to Mummy and Daddy then, I'm warning you now, don't fight at—wait a second.' Ed began to smile. 'You . . . you don't have a mum and dad!'

Without warning, Jack's normally calm and pleasant demeanour slowly changed, and his face contorted in an all-consuming anger—his nostrils flaring, his eyes flashing and closing into slits, his mouth quivering, drooling, and slurring; words that were unintelligible came spewing into space like a volcano releasing its pent-up emotions into the darkness.

His hands closed into fists, and he crouched forward, daring him to repeat the words that had torn his heart into fragments, that had dashed all his expectations of 'happy ever after'. He no longer cared what his martial arts teacher had taught him. He no longer cared about self-control. And so he didn't wait!

Then he let go with a right uppercut to the head that sent Ed flying from one side of the room to the other at what seemed like the speed of light. Ed's body made contact with the opposite wall, and he slid to the floor like a sack of potatoes.

When he came to, he asked, 'What was that for?'

Ed got up and stung Jack's face with a rock-hard punch. And in a matter of seconds, they were stuck together like glue, punching each other.

I could go on, my dear reader; however, it would only get gruesome, and I believe I have answered your question.

Little did they know, Jack's younger sister, Lily, had followed Jack downstairs and had witnessed the fist fight. She didn't care about Ed, but what if her brother got hurt? Lily had decided she was going to defend him no matter what.

Lily plucked up all her courage and got ready to speak.

'Leave Jack alone, you big hairy ape!'

Suddenly, Ed turned. 'What did you say, you little freak?'

'You heard me!'

Jack was relieved that he didn't have to take on Ed alone; he was also mildly embarrassed by the concept of having to have his eleven-year-old sister standing up for him. Suddenly, Jack took his gaze off Lily. Ed was charging at his sister with a fist as solid as granite.

Without hesitation, Jack jumped in between the two and grabbed Ed's fist. Then and there, he twisted his hand and threw him against the sofa, waiting for a reaction. Ed was speechless.

'That's what I thought,' Jack whispered, just loud enough to be heard.

He seized Lily's hand and dragged her back up the stairs to the filthy, sordid attic that was Jack and Lily's bedroom. He scolded her for getting herself involved.

Jack had no idea what had just happened and why he had suddenly lost his temper, but the boy had one thing in mind: he hated this place and he was going to get out. He could escape, perhaps? If so, he'd have to do it in the dead of the night when both Uncle Alistair and Aunt Mary were asleep. Maybe he could call one of his friends and stay there for a few days until he was ready to come back. He could even go back to the care home for a few days. Involuntarily, he reached for his diary, ripped a page out, and began to write his escape plan. That was the option he had chosen, and that was the option he was going to stick with.

He wrote and wrote until finally he heard a little whisper in his head telling him to stop. He lay his head against the pillow and went to sleep.

Suddenly, he woke up. He had heard a noise. Jack sat bolt upright as sweat trickled down his forehead and down to his bare shoulders. He had always slept semi-nude. The noise had sounded quite loud. He looked to his side, and to his shock, Lily had her eyes wide open and was staring directly at him. She held a piece of paper. Emblazoned upon it were three words.

My Escape Plan

She stared him directly in the eye. It hit him like a moving car as he remembered his last sentence. It had stated that he was going to have to leave his sister behind.

'Fine, fine,' he said. 'Look, I'm sorry. You can come if you want.'

Jack thought that by saying this, it would erase the look of horror on her face. All it did was make it worse. He couldn't stand watching his sister upset. She was all he had, and he couldn't possibly lose her too. Maybe he should've forgotten about the escape and just carried on with his life normally. Unfortunately, that option didn't even cross his mind until later on. He would've most definitely preferred to leave the prison and keep his distance from his mother's side of the family. He had no one to confide in when fear began to talk to him. Lily was that person. How could he leave her behind? Jack's best mate, Dylan, was in hospital. He had no one to talk to. His life was miserable, and he had been missing school more and more. Everyone had started to bully him when they found out that his mother and father had died. He knew he couldn't leave Lily yet; he was so close to her.

CHAPTER 2

Oops, I Didn't Think of That

'But I don't want to leave this place', sobbed Lily. 'Uncle Alistair and Aunt Mary have been so kind to us. They let us take refuge with them while no one else would accept us.'

'Yeah, yeah, whatever,' Jack said. 'They beat us up every night before bed and when we wake up just for the fun of it. And what about Edward? He's been *so* kind to us, right?'

Lily lay her head back down and stayed still as if she, for once, was actually thinking about what Jack had just said. Suddenly, her facial expression changed as if she had detected a massive flaw in Jack's plan, a fatal flaw. 'Okay then, Mister I-Have-Everything-Planned, even if we do manage to escape, where exactly would we go?'

Jack strained his mind to its limit. He hadn't thought about that. 'I'll . . . I'll find somewhere,' he said, trying to stay optimistic and look confident.

Young Jack had not anticipated this flaw. It was like a missing puzzle piece of the one-thousand-word jigsaws that he used to play with his mum when he was little. *No*, Jack thought, *I have to stay strong*. He decided he wasn't going to let thoughts about his dead mum and dad drag him down.

Lily could see that her older brother had had everything planned even before that day. On the floor, placed quite closely to the bed, was a big bag in which Jack had packed his clothes and belongings. It had also seemed that Jack had predicted Lily was going to want to come as well; therefore, placed closely to his bag was Lily's bag as well.

Of course she wanted to assist her brother in any way possible, but assisting him with an escape? Now that's what Lily would've called going too far. She turned around, and to her horror, Jack was gone.

She ran down the stairs, hoping she'd be able to catch up with him, but unfortunately, *she* was caught up with instead.

'Where'd you think you're going?' asked a bewildered Edward. 'Oh, I get it.' Ed was now smirking, and Lily didn't like where this was going. 'You're running away just like your swine of a brother! You know, my dear cousin Lily, Mum and Dad are easily annoyed, especially when they're woken up early.'

'Don't you dare, you—' Lily was interrupted by a massive noise echoing down the stairs. It was her aunt and uncle. Lily was definitely going to get a punishment from her uncle and aunt, and just before Alistair and Mary could catch a glimpse of her, she flipped a gesture involving a specific finger. She grabbed hold of her bag, making sure no one could see her, and then dumped a melted packet of Cadbury's Dairy Milk chocolate all over Edward's face. Then she began her journey looking for her brother.

'Oh, Edward! You ate *all* the chocolate!' screamed Aunt Mary, almost deafening Lily.

'What's got into you, boy?' Alistair bellowed as he took out his belt.

Lily's legs felt like jelly. She had walked for what seemed like an eternity and was staring at what looked like a man in his late thirties. He had shaggy black hair draped across his face. Lily had a good idea about exactly who this man could be; she had a very good idea.

'It can't be,' she whispered to herself.

She looked closely and realised that just above his nose, under his left eye, he had the exact same shape and size of scar that Jack had across his cheek.

She waited and waited. Finally, he spoke.

'Jack Stone will die,' he said, maintaining that devilishly petrifying smile of his.

Again, Lily waited for more.

'So will Lily . . .'

CHAPTER 3

Say Hello to Leon

Lily woke up in the arms of her older brother while a teenage boy, who seemed about Jack's age, crouched next to her. The boy had short, close-cropped ginger hair. His eyes were sky blue, and he wore a devilish grin.

'Told you she'd be all right. "But what if she never comes back?"' he said, mimicking her brother.

Lily couldn't help but laugh. The boy seemed very good at impressions.

'Look, Leon, I was just worried about my sister. Do you have a problem with that?'

The boy whom Jack had called Leon ignored Jack's question and turned to Lily. 'Are you OK? Your brother and I found you outside the park. I'm Leon, Leon Ramirez. I've been sent here by Zeus to spy on you to see if you two are ready.'

'Ready?' Lily asked, confused.

'Now calm down. You and Jack are godlings, and so am I actua—'

'Wait, what?'

'You know? Godlings?' The boy called Leon sighed, as if this question wasn't new to him at all. 'Okay. Thousands of years ago, the

Three Brothers, Zeus, Poseidon, and Hades, decided to take small fractals of their godly, powerful souls and teleport them into three human warriors. One warrior for Zeus, one warrior for Poseidon, and one warrior for Hades. The three warriors that received the powers became godlings, the very first in history. Since then, the future generations of the three warriors possessed the same powers. One day, the other Olympians decided to do the same as the Three Brothers, and now you can possess powers of different gods too.'

'Yeah. Leon is a Zeus godling,' Jack interrupted.

Lily was surprised to find out that even her older brother, Jack, knew more than her about this subject. Usually, it was the other way round. Then again, *her* brother had spent more time with Leon than her.

'How long have I been out?'

'About three hours. Could've been longer if Leon decided to not help,' explained Jack.

Lily was curious. She had to know more about this godling stuff, but she was worried that the truth might be linked to her parents' death.

Well, my reader, I think you have probably guessed the truth about her parents and the truth about the man she had seen before she collapsed. But just in case you haven't, I'll tell you now. Both of Lily's parents were godlings. Daniel—a Hermes. Tamara—an Aphrodite. Oh, and by the way, the man that Lily saw was, in fact, the cause of her parents' accident. Anyway, back to the story.

Lily cleared her throat and opened her mouth to speak, but her question (Does Zeus do anything else?) was interrupted by Leon answering, 'Zeus is the camp leader of Camp Nikas, the only place safe in the world for godlings, and before you ask, yeah, he is the lightning-and-thunder Greek god dude. I can't wait 'til you meet him.'

'H-how did you know my question?'

'Telekinesis and telepathy. You get taught that by Hecate,' Leon said, those two sentences as casual as they could be.

'So anyway, when do we start our journey for Nikas?' Lily asked. The question was directed at Leon; however, it was answered by Jack.

'The first of August.'

Lily reached for her phone; she had placed it in the back pocket of her jeans. She felt for it. It wasn't in its original place. Worried, Lily checked all her pockets. No result. It was gone.

'Hey!'

Lily looked up, and she couldn't believe her eyes. There, in front of her, sat Leon holding his hand out. Lily looked closer; she began to inspect with great scrutiny exactly what was in Leon's hand. Eventually, Lily realised that Leon was holding her phone. Lily snatched the phone out of her hand and shot Leon a dirty look.

'I could've done that myself!' Lily mumbled.

She entered her PIN code, which unlocked her phone, and checked the time and date. It said 03.37 Tuesday 28 July, meaning they had four days left until the journey to Nikas. Leon had explained about some of the teachers and which children they'd have to look out for.

Lily was worried about some of the consequences of travelling to Nikas, and she couldn't stop thinking about the scrawny man she had seen before she had blacked out. On his right forearm, he had a strange tattoo shaped like lightning. She traced it across the palm of her hand and then drew it on a piece of paper. The pattern on the paper quickly vanished, but Lily knew she needn't worry. She had memorised it. She looked back at her palm. The symbol she had traced was suddenly darker and looked as if she had written it in a marker pen. Next to it was a word written in ancient Greek. Lily could read Greek (thanks to her teacher Mrs Carter), but unfortunately, her knowledge was very little. Luckily, she knew enough to understand. Her palm had read ⚡ πέτρα. It was the Greek word for 'stone'.

The reason that Jack and Lily's surname was placed close to the lightning bolt is a whole other story. But those who are more astute among you might be able to guess in this story. I'll give you a hint. The lightning bolt signifies the king of the gods, Zeus. Have you got it yet?

Lily shook off the fear, walked up to Leon, and pulled him aside. She waited for Leon to speak, but since he took too long, Lily decided to start talking.
'So while I was out, exactly what did you say to Jack about Mum and Dad?'
Leon stayed quiet; Lily began to worry exactly what Leon had told her brother.
'Oh, don't worry. I didn't tell him anything about your parents. And you—'
'Good, 'cause I know everything that happened. It was that guy I saw before I blacked out. Um. . . what's his name again . . . uh . . . ? Crunches?'
'Shut up!' Leon said, probably loud enough for Jack to hear. 'You saw Kronos? Do you know how dangerous this is? Listen up— people who see Kronos are unlucky, very unlucky. People who see Kronos . . . Oh, no. I'm sorry.'
'Tell me!' Lily insisted.
'People who see Kronos usually die.'

CHAPTER 4

Camp Nikas

The four days until the journey to Nikas passed like seconds, and within those 'seconds', Lily couldn't stop thinking about what Leon had said. She'd decided she'd have to forget it with all the commotion going on. But she just couldn't.

Jack, on the other hand, was having a great time. He had just found out he was a godling and was taking the news much better than his younger sister. Jack spent every hour of this time thinking about Nikas. Finally, the day they were leaving arrived.

All of a sudden, Jack grabbed his trunk and began stuffing everything in it. What if they didn't make it in time? Would they still accept him?

Leon walked up to Jack. 'You okay?'

'This stupid packing is taking too long!'

Leon sighed. 'Get out of the way.'

Jack did as he was told.

'*Lapio!*' Leon waved his hand and conjured the packing spell. All of Jack's possessions flew into his trunk; his clothes were neatly folded and put into the trunk.

'Mum was always good at them spells. Taught me some,' added Leon.

Jack stared, mystified, and said, 'You have to teach me that magic!'

'Sorry,' Leon began. 'You don't get taught that stuff until third year.'

Jack suddenly looked upset. 'Anyway, how do we get there?'

'We'll have to use the Portalis Charm.'

'Cool, more magic!'

Lily stood there annoyed. Jack was acting like a three-year-old.

'Can we get on with this?' she asked.

Leon explained that they had to hold hands and not let go until the magic was done.

'Ready, steady, and *Portalio*!'

In front of the trio appeared a massive purple gap in the air. The purple gap must've had an extremely strong gravitational pull because it began to suck everything in. The Stones and Leon had a hard time trying to avoid being sucked in.

'Okay,' Leon said, trying his best to be heard over the whooshing sound coming from the portal. 'When I say *go*, all together we will shout "Portalio, Cendre!" Oh, and remember we must hold hands. Cendre is an ancient city packed with godlings and is a very large city. When we get there, try not to get lost. One, two, three, and *go*!'

The trio hollered the two words and leapt into the portal, Jack with a very tight grip on the handle of his trunk. Both Jack and Lily felt as if they had run around in a circle a hundred times, mainly Lily. Jack tried his best to stay still, but in the portal that Leon had conjured, there was no way he was going to stop moving. *Bang!*

All of a sudden, they found themselves standing outside what looked like a school. It seemed as if the school had been expecting them as over the entrance was a huge banner which had, printed in bold, italicised writing, the words:

CAMP NIKAS

WELCOME, JACK AND LILY STONE

Both Lily and Jack were shocked to see that their arrival had actually been noticed. Seldom had they ever been cared about. All around the siblings stood a multitude of teens which seemed to go on forever. Suddenly, the crowd of children split into two, making a large gap for the Stones to walk through—or at least that's what they thought. In fact, the gap was for a completely different person. A man, who seemed to have materialised right at that moment, walked towards the pair. He wore a large plate of armour that went from his Adam's apple down to his shins; on his feet, he wore a pair of leather-soled sandals, and he had a large amount of hair that looked as if it had been unattended to for millennia. To add to that, he also wore an unnecessary amount of facial hair.

'Nice shoes,' whistled Jack.

'Oh, yeah,' the bearded man replied. 'Leather soles. Good-quality straps. Arch support. These shoes will last a lifetime. Anyway, Jack, Lily, I'm Zeus, camp leader here at Nikas. I am also, as you probably know, god of thunder and lightning and overall god of the sky.'

'So you're the famous Zeus. Nice to meet you,' Jack said.

The two shook hands and then, for absolutely no reason whatsoever, decided to headbutt each other.

'Boys,' Lily muttered to herself.

'And you must be Lily.'

Lily and Zeus shook hands, and the two followed the god to the end of the large gap the crowd had made. Zeus had shown the two to two separate thrones. And in a matter of seconds, Jack and Lily were sitting upon two separate thrones with invisible servants feeding them unnecessarily large amounts of fruit. They felt like royalty.

'Loyal godlings, I present to you two of our newest members here at Camp Nikas. We will welcome them with great benevolence and not show any disrespect to our newly recruited members. I am talking to you especially, Enya,' announced Zeus.

The girl who must've been Enya rolled her eyes, and she stuck her tongue out. 'Oh yes, almost forgot. Their protector, Leon, will need a helper, so if there are any volunteers, please raise your hand.'

Jack wasn't listening to a single word coming out of Zeus's mouth. Instead, he was examining the campers he would be staying with. Suddenly, Jack caught a glimpse of a strange-looking girl, strange because she looked like an older version of his sister and, apart from her brown hair, a younger version of his mother. She looked up and caught him staring. She mouthed *What*.

He tried to ignore her and listen to what Zeus was saying, but no matter how hard he tried, he couldn't get her out of his head. Her beautifully braided warm-mocha-coloured hair cascaded down her shoulders like uncoiling fluid streams. Her features were so delicate they could've been carved out of ice. He had to find out who she was.

On the other hand, Lily was loving Camp Nikas a lot more than she had expected and felt no other emotion apart from gaiety and euphoria. She was not even bothered by what Leon had told her four days ago. She couldn't believe that she had considered staying with the Sterlings.

However, if one thing was bothering both of the Stones, it was that girl Enya. Even Leon had warned them about her. Enya had short choppy black hair that fell across her eyes like stray streaks of charcoal. She smiled at the siblings as if warning them that if they made one mistake she would finish them. She was like the female version of Ed.

The next day was when the real training began. Their two trainers for sword fighting were Leon and, since no one else had volunteered, Zeus. Jack was hoping that he would get a chance to see that girl he had seen yesterday. If only she had volunteered.

'Jack. Jack!'

Jack suddenly turned and realised that he was daydreaming.

'Um. . . yes, sir?'

Zeus gestured towards the sword ring. Jack analysed his opponent. It was the same girl from yesterday.

'You want me to fight her?'

'Well, duh!' she interrupted.

'You know, Zeus. I would just like you to know that I have absolutely no problem beating a girl. I am what you would call in French *le meilleur*.'

Jack walked into the ring and did ten press-ups. He then unsheathed his sword and waited for the camp leader's command to begin.

'On the left, we have the American Alexa Rivera, leader, head counsellor, and trainee representative of the Athena godlings. Not to mention winner of the Godling of the Year award five times in a row!'

Nearly all the campers began to chant Alexa's name.

Rounds of applause and calling erupted from the crowds.

Zeus continued, 'On the right, we have the Australian Jack Stone, future warrior godling, a beginner in sword fighting and a waiter in the Waiter godlings.'

Zeus was probably expecting the godlings to cheer for Jack as well, but instead, everyone went into an awkward moment of complete silence, which rarely happened here at Camp Nikas.

Jack began to blush. His secret was out. He'd always tried to hide his Australian accent even at home. It was mainly because he had been teased at school about it. His mum and dad were English, but he had lived most of his early life in Australia.

Zeus cleared his throat. 'Let the battle commence!'

Alexa jumped in with the first strike; her knife slashed across Jack's face. It seemed that the girl whom Jack now knew was called Alexa had drawn the first sheds of blood.

'Whoa!' he said. 'You guys take training way too seriously. You need to calm down.'

Jack swiped his sword blindly. Suddenly he realised that it was going for her face. He tried to pull the sword back but he didn't need to. Rapidly fast, Alexa ducked and slashed her knife across Jack's legs.

'Come on, Stone. Get up.' She said his surname as if it disgusted her (which it probably did).

'Please, please. *Please!* You're hurting me,' Jack cried. He couldn't take it anymore. Alexa charged in, her knife ready to stab him.

'*No!*'

Jack's vision suddenly became blurry. He had heard that voice before, Leon's voice. He knew what had happened. It was all clear now. But if Jack was right . . .

'*Stop!*'

In front of him was his best friend on his knees.

Leon had taken the knife for him.

CHAPTER 5

A Cursed Blade

Jack stood there, staring at his wounded friend. He couldn't believe what just happened. He looked up at Alexa, his eyes red with anger. He began to charge. His hair went wild as his feet began to move involuntarily. He grabbed his sword while running.

His eyes were glaring with menace; he was ready for anything. He was only a few metres away now and imagined the pain she would be going through when this was over. It would serve her right. She had killed his best friend here. Lily stared at her brother. What had he turned into? Leon was shocked at Jack.

'No!' Leon screamed, his hand reaching out for Jack to stop while the other was clutched over his sternum.

Jack came to an abrupt halt. Assiduously, he turned and stared at Leon. He stared at Alexa and then at Leon. What was he doing? No. He was going to kill her.

'She . . . she could've killed you!'

'Or she could've killed *you*!' the boy croaked.

Alexa stood there, her mouth wide open as if it were the first time she had ever been scared. Jack dropped his sword onto the ground, turned around, and stared at the girl.

'You are sick. You are so sick. I'm not even going to bother talking to you any more.'

He turned to Zeus. 'You ought to do something about that waste of space.'

He walked to the Waiter cabin and sat on his bed. He wanted to go back and apologise, but something was holding him back. After Leon had taken the knife for him, he had seen a man with shaggy dark hair and a scar similar to his own under the man's eye. Jack looked at his arm; the tattoo was still there. Of course, it had always been since he was born with it. He lay his head on the pillow and went to sleep.

Meanwhile, Lily stood within the crowd of godlings, gobsmacked. Who was that she had seen charging at Alexa? Her brother had turned into some kind of monster. Very rarely did the boy lose his temper. He needed to calm down. But then Lily understood why he was angry. If someone had done that to Mo, she would probably have done the same. She would leave him for a few minutes and then go back to check on him. Finally, those minutes passed.

'Jack!' she cried, sprinting at top speed into their room. 'Jack?'

She realised that Jack was sleeping. He looked calm and peaceful, nothing like he had a few minutes before.

'Oh,' she said. She walked up to her older brother, who was asleep, and kissed him on the forehead.

'Love you, Jack. And by the way, Leon's fine. He was healed pretty quick actually.'

Lily realised it was kind of stupid, standing there talking to her brother who was asleep. She turned around, walked to her bed, pulled her blanket over her, and was ready to go to sleep. But she just couldn't.

My reader, you have now witnessed the love and the strong bond between the brother and sister, the main characters of this very true story. I would like to tell you now that their love plays a very important part in this very true story.

'Lily. Lily! Come on, it's eleven o'clock in the morning and you're still asleep!'

'Um . . . uh,' Lily stammered. 'Actually, I'm half asleep.'

'Whatever. Are you going to wake up?'

Lily looked up. She had hoped to see Jack; instead, she saw Alexa looming over her.

'What are you doing here?' she asked, sitting up.

'Don't worry,' she said. 'Everything's fine with me, and Jack and Leon's fully recovered. The Apollo godlings healed him.'

'Jack was probably pleased to hear that news, eh?'

'He was!'

Lily couldn't believe her brother and Alexa were friends. After what happened yesterday, it didn't make sense to Lily that Alexa and Jack were back to being friends again. *Hang on a sec*, Lily thought. *Were they* ever *friends? Whatever.*

Lily grabbed her Stax SR 009 headphones and changed into her favourite jeans and her 'I ♥ London' T-shirt and ran out of her bedroom.

'Oops, forgot my phone,' Lily suddenly noticed.

'Lily,' said Alexa as soon as Lily began to walk back out the door.

'Yes?'

'*Katharioso!*' Alexa's voice echoed across the room, and all of a sudden, Lily's hair was neat and tidy; her teeth felt fresh like the feeling you get after brushing your teeth, and it had seemed her perfume and lipstick had applied themselves magically.

'Wow, thanks, Alexa,' said Lily examining herself. 'Now I can walk out looking decent again!'

'It's fine, really.'

Finally Lily walked out of the cabin, listening to her headphones. If she had found her iPod, she would've probably left her headphones back inside. But yet again, it had seemed that Jack had borrowed (or stolen) it again. She was listening to her favourite song, 'Shake It Off' by Taylor Swift. She had always liked that song and had memorised all the words. The only problem was that Lily couldn't sing to save her life. She began to whisper the lyrics so that no-one could hear her shrieks, 'I stay up too late | got nothing in my brain, | that's what people say, | that's what people say. | I go on too many—'

'Hey, Lils!' shouted Jack, interrupting Lily's moment of peace and tranquillity. 'You might wanna come over here!'

'It's "You might *want to* come over here", Jack,' she muttered to herself as quietly as she could.

It was obvious to Lily that her brother Jack had always talked like that. He was the worst at grammar in the world. He had got a D in anything that involved spelling or reading. But then again, Jack *was* dyslexic. The only thing he was really and truly good at was probably football. He would probably make a great footballer. She turned in the direction of her brother, awaiting his so-called surprise. All of a sudden, she caught a glimpse of a dark-tanned boy about her age high-fiving Jack. She looked closer.

'Mo?' Lily asked herself. *No,* she thought, *it can't be. Can it?* Now she was certain. One hundred per cent certain. Her headphones fell across her shoulder as if they were reacting to what she had just seen.

'Mo!' she screamed, charging towards him. She pounced at him with a hug.

'Lily,' he said. 'Calm down!'

'What are you doing here?' she asked, a wide grin on her face.

'I'm a Waiter. I've come for my first year here at Camp Nikas.'

'Same!' she said as she pounced at him with another hug. 'I've missed you so much. So much!'

Zeus passed by the gate where Jack, Lily, and Mo were standing.

'Zeus!' Lily cried. 'Mo and I have to be put together! I'm begging you.'

'Well, young lady. We shall see tonight.' He winked at her as if he was almost confirming it.

'Hey, anyway, what are you listening to?'

'"Shake It Off". Taylor Swift!'

''Cause the players gonna play, play, play, and the haters gonna hate, hate, hate, but baby I'm just gonna shake, shake, shake. Shake it off!' they sung together.

'Here, come on. Let's go to my room.'

And so the two went to Mo's room in the Waiters' cabin.

Meanwhile, Jack stayed behind, staring at the two. When suddenly . . .

'Ahem,' Alexa cleared her throat. 'So that's the famous Mo. Cool. Oh, by the way, your sister's got good style in music. Wait a second, does your sister have that song? "Style"?' Alexa began to murmur the words to the song.

'Just my luck,' Jack muttered to himself, as he began walking away to his next lesson. Jack couldn't wait to find out where he'd be staying; he had hoped to be staying with the Ares or the Zeus guys.

Finally, after days, the time had come for the sorting to begin. They went through many children before they reached the trio.

'Mo Lawson. Stand.'

Mo stood, obeying Zeus's command. 'Yes, sir.'

Zeus stayed quiet for a while, cleared his throat, and got ready to speak. 'Apollo!'

Mo walked to the Apollos, hoping and praying to Apollo that Lily would be an Apollo as well.

'Jack Stone. Stand.'

'Yes, sir,' he said, his voice trembling.

'Poseidon!'

Jack celebrated by doing a backflip followed by a cartwheel and then taking his shirt off.

'Inappropriate, Jack. Inappropriate.'

'Sorry, sir,' he said walking to his cabin, a wide grin on his face.

'Lily Stone. Stand.'

Lily was the only one out of all the campers who didn't reply with a 'Yes, sir'.

'Ahem. . .' he cleared his throat as he circled around her. 'Difficult. Very difficult. You could do well in my cabin. Very well. But that would mean you would get separated from young Lawson.' He stared at her, his decision made. . .

All of a sudden, Zeus fell to the ground. His voice became harsh and raspy.

'It's here. He's here.'

'Who, sir, who's here?' asked Lily as she leapt towards him, trying to stop his godly blood, *ichor*, from flowing.

'The cursed blade, the prophecy. . .'

'WHO'S HERE?' screamed Lily, now desperate for answers.

'It has to be the cursed blade'

'I SAID WHO'S HERE?'

'Father.'

CHAPTER 6

The Son of Minos

'Quick, get someone—now!' screamed Lily as tears streamed down her eyes. She was desperate now.

Jack had never seen his sister so angry. He ran towards his sister and held her tight; he pulled her away from Zeus.

'Listen,' he said, his voice ragged. 'Stay away from him and go and get Mo. Tell the Poseidons that your my sister and stay with them. Mo and I can handle this.'

'No!' Lily insisted. 'I'm staying with you.'

Jack paused for a while and stared at the panicking godlings. The fire that Zeus had lit with his lightning bolt was spreading rapidly.

'Okay,' he managed. 'But bring Mo with you. Now that he's been sorted, he's got some essential powers an Apollo godling needs.'

Lily ran back to the Apollo cabin to fetch Mo, but once she was in the cabin, she got locked in.

'Jack, you liar!'

'I'm sorry,' Jack said. 'But I'm not losing you two as well.'

Jack ran back to the centre of the battle; it was complete chaos. He hadn't wanted to lock her in, but he had to protect her and Mo. He rushed to Zeus.

Meanwhile, Lily and Mo kept banging on the door, crying for help.

'Oh, just forget it,' said Mo as he fell on his bed.

'You're probably right.'

Lily and Mo spent an awkward moment in complete silence (well, except for the shouting and screaming outside). Lily and Mo couldn't believe all the drama stirring up in their lives. Since school was the place where they had first met, Lily decided to talk about that.

'So', Lily began, 'how's school without me?'

Mo didn't reply; his eyes were fixed upon the window opposite his bed. Lily could see something was wrong with him. He kept staring into the air. Lily had guessed that something bad was about to happen. But what, she had no idea.

'Mo? Mo!'

Still no reply.

'Mo, are you okay?'

Then she looked up. The same filthy, shaggy, untidy man Lily had seen before she had lost consciousness loomed over the window. He began to walk through the wall, as if he were just another lonely apparition from *Harry Potter*. In a matter of seconds, he was sitting on Lewis Daniels's bed, which was, unfortunately, the bed directly in front of them.

'Lily,' he coughed, smirking like he had never smirked before. 'We meet again.'

Lily stood up but was pulled back down by Mo, who, mouth still open wide with shock, unexpectedly leapt at Lily with a hug. Lily put her arm around Mo and began, 'Listen here, Crunchys! I know you killed our parents. Stay away from me and Jack!'

'And me!' Mo squeaked.

'You heard him,' Lily insisted.

'Is that so?'

My reader, the news that Lily was about to hear was going to both break her heart and fill her with hope.

'Well, young lady, I think you'd like to know that'—he cleared his throat—'I have no intention to touch you or your loser of a brother. I don't even know who Mo is, and I, unfortunately, have not killed your parents. They're in Tartarus with me.'

'*Liar!*' Lily screamed. 'My parents are dead!'

Just after that, Lily began to feel strange, as if she were doubting herself. But she couldn't be, could she? Her parents must be dead; everyone had said so. But what if they were lying to her? What if they thought they were dead too?

Jack stood still. He had heard something strange and very peculiar. He had overhead his sister talking about his parents. About his parents' death. But why would she?

He sprinted towards the door and kicked it open. The sprinting helped him recall old memories of him chasing after the ball, and the kicking reminded him of smashing the ball into the net. The door smashed, sending pieces of debris flying everywhere. When it had all calmed down, he couldn't believe his eyes. It was the same man he had seen a few days ago after fighting Alexa.

'You?' he exclaimed.

'Wait a sec.' Lily was unaware that Jack knew who this man was. 'You know him?'

'Oh, I know him, and I'm gonna kill him! Like he did to Mum and Dad.'

Kronos sighed. 'O, mighty Ouranos, lend me your strength. Your parents are alive!' He over pronounced the last word so that it sounded as if he were saying *ay-lie-va*.

He showed the three a vision of their parents being dragged across the floor by what looked like the old Greek Titan. What was his name? Energy? No. Hyper? No. Hyperion. That was his name. Suddenly, the image dematerialised into thin air.

'Why didn't you kill him when he first came in?' Jack asked.

'Do you ever pay attention? He is a Titan. Titan with a capital *T*. And Titans are immortal.'

Lily couldn't understand anything that was going on. Were her mum and dad really still alive? And even if they were, could she and Jack really get them back? She had so many questions going on in her head; she didn't know what she was going to do.

'You know what—it doesn't matter. I'm going to bed. You guys should too.'

As Lily, Jack, and Mo began walking over dead bodies to get to their beds, they suddenly realised something strange. Across their cabin doors, written in blood, were the words 'I am the Son of Minos, and you are my victims.'

CHAPTER 7

The Minotaur

'Victims? Son of Minos?' Jack asked himself, staring at the blood-written words as fear began to cascade like cold water down his face. 'That's the Minotaur, right?'

'Well, yeah, but he wasn't exactly the son of Minos. Minos never had any children. Asterion, known as the Minotaur, was the son of Pasiphae and the Marathonian Bull, Minos's prize bull. Eventually, he got killed by Theseus, demigod son of Poseidon, Aegus, and Aethra. So why he's alive now completely baffles me.'

'You know what?' said Mo. 'I'm gonna be completely honest with you—I think you should be an Athena.'

'I hate Athena,' Lily replied.

Immediately an owl flew down from an olive tree and bit Lily's finger.

'Ow! Sorry, Athena.'

The owl tweeted as if to say, 'That's what you get!' and flew away.

Suddenly the trio realised that Zeus was no longer sprawled across the floor. In fact, they couldn't see him anywhere; they had figured that he probably had gone back up to Mount Olympus in his nice, cosy god-size bed. Mo was loving this. Every injured or dead person he would see would suddenly come back to life, stroll to their bed, and fall asleep, probably waking up fine the next day.

The next few weeks were a lot less eventful. Lily had managed to settle in fine with the other Aphrodite godlings. She had even made a few friends. It was a Friday evening, and the banquet had just finished. The evening banquets were some of the very few times that Jack and Lily got to see each other. Just after the banquet, Lily went back into her cabin. She slumped down on her bed and thought. She thought about how she had actually got into this mess. The very beginning.

'Oh yeah,' she said to herself. 'I ran away from home.'

Without warning, Lily began to hear footsteps.

'Talking to yourself? First sign of madness.'

'Shut up.'

It was Harper. Harper was one of Lily's many friends here at Camp Nikas, but out of all of them, she was, by far, the best. She even beat Mo. But of course Lily wouldn't tell him that. Harper was an American girl with hair that was always changing style. Today, she was wearing her hair in a bun that lay still on the top of her head. Her hair was blond with the occasional streak of brown running through it. Lily had suspected that she had had it highlighted, but according to her, it was all natural.

'So what's wrong?'

'I think I'm going to need to leave this place.'

'Well, I hope you don't. But if you do, I'm gonna teach you a trick that might come in handy.'

'I'm listening.'

'I'm gonna teach you hypnosis.'

Harper spent hours tutoring Lily. She explained that you looked the victim in the eye and quietly clicked your fingers while stating what you wanted.

'Thanks, Harper.'

'You're welcome. Remember, whenever you need me, just give me a call.'

Lily walked out of her cabin and called out to Zeus, and a few minutes later, she could see a goddess, probably Hera, telling him to be careful and to watch out for any danger.

'So', Zeus said, 'what seems to be the problem?'

The Stones and Mo explained everything. Zeus couldn't believe what he was hearing; the three could see it on his face.

'No,' he insisted. 'You can't go.'

'But thousands of innocent people will die if we don't,' Jack cleverly pointed out because that's the kind of smart person he was.

'I said you can't go!' Zeus hollered as thunder began to roar and lightning began to crash down. 'Last time this happened, my. . .'

Zeus's voice had begun to soften to a whisper. 'Look, I can't force you to stay, but if you're going, if you're really going, then at least take Leon and Alexa with you, but don't make the same mistake he made.'

'Who?' Lily asked. 'The same mistake *who* made?'

'Look, are you going or not?'

'Yes.'

'Well, pack up, and don't ask any questions. Meet me outside the gates tomorrow at five, and bring Alexa and Leon with you. And by the way, Lily, you're an Aphrodite. And please don't anger Athena any more—she threatened that in the next king of the god's election she'd vote for Hades. I mean, *Hades*. Seriously.'

Finally the time came. Lily, Jack, and Mo had hardly any sleep. The three got up and got changed. They had told Alexa and Leon to meet them outside the gates with their suitcases ready and had explained everything to them, which took a rather long time. Jack,

Lily, and Mo had found the others already waiting for them outside, talking about the adventure that awaited them. Lily wore faded jeans, hiking boots, and a fleece snowboarding jacket with her new emoji rucksack. Her chocolate-brown hair fell down her shoulders, with thin strands braided down the side.

Everyone could now see why she was an Aphrodite godling now; everyone was staring at her.

'What?' Lily asked shyly. 'Can we get on with this?'

'Ahem.' Zeus cleared his throat. 'I see you are all packed and ready to go. Not the best godlings I would've chose to go on an adventure together. A Poseidon, an Aphrodite, an Apollo, an Athena, and a Zeus. But, well, good luck. Okay, so, Alexa and Leon, I trust you've brought your swords and shields,' he said as he handed a sword and a shield to Jack and a bow and some arrows to Mo. He then handed a knife and a shield to Lily.

Lily looked at her knife. It was small, but its serrated edges looked like they could do a lot of damage.

'And I trust you all have your sleeping bags and tents?'

Everyone tapped their rucksacks and, one by one, hugged the camp leader.

'Bye,' they all said in unison as they began walking out of the gate.

Zeus wiped his eyes and whispered, 'Bye. . .'

The first three days were probably the most difficult. After hours of walking, dusk had finally fallen, and they decided to put up the tents and take out their sleeping bags. The boys took one tent, and the girls took the other. Already, during the first few days, the five had used most of their food supplies, and they could only hope that their journey would end sooner rather than later. They had decided to sleep by the mountains. And every now and then, Jack would go out of the tent staring straight at the mountains with a crest-fallen face. And sometimes Lily would go into the boys' tent to wish her brother goodnight.

The fourth day was when they began to encounter trouble.

Everyone stopped straight in their tracks, staring at the situation that was going on behind Leon. Leon, however, didn't have a clue about the current scenario.

'Come on, then,' Leon said. 'That Minotaur's not going to kill himself, is he? Although it *would* save us a lot of trouble if he did.'

Leon turned to keep on walking, and suddenly, the boy realised why everyone was standing as still and rigid as four lamp posts. He decided to shut up. There, roaring right at him, was *the* Nemean Lion. It stood there, its immense body directed at him while its tail began to wave aggressively. It was hungry. Ravenous. There was no way the team could pass the lion without any major injuries.

'Here, kitty, kitty,' Alexa began, trying to distract the lion, slowly circling it. She reached for her backpack and pulled out a packet of crisps. Roast chicken. Hopefully, the lion would smell the aroma and would dash in the direction of the crisps. The others had to give it to her; Alexa was brave.

'Alexa, you're the Athena. What's so special about this lion?' Jack asked, not worried at all.

'It's the Nemean Lion. It was killed by Hercules as his first task given to him by Erikstheus. Its skin is unnaturally thick, and it was said that Hercules's sword snapped against its body while he was trying to stab it. Hercules killed it by strangling it.'

'That's it. I've had enough.' Jack threw his rucksack on to the floor and charged at the lion.

'No!' Alexa shouted.

He pounced on its neck while everyone was staring and began to ride it like a horse.

He counted to three and then twisted its body so now the lion was lying with its back towards the floor. The lion was lying over him, and Jack's face suddenly turned red as he couldn't breathe. He drove his heel into its groin (he knew how much that hurt, thanks to Uncle Al) and then placed his lower arm across its neck. He applied so much pressure that it could've killed any man, but this lion was nothing like any man and so it stayed alive. He let go. Again the lion came charging at him; he jumped on its back and then got ready for the next dangerous move.

He took his whole right arm and placed it to the side of the lion's face while it was charging. Suddenly, it seized his arm with its dagger-like teeth and pierced into his arm; he howled with pain. Nevertheless, he knew his plan had to go on. He wrapped his arm around the lion and put it in a headlock (please do not try this at home!). He began to apply so much pressure he fell off the lion's back and began running beside it. Soon he barged his shoulder into it, and they both fell on to the floor, synchronised apart from one thing: one of them was dead. Although Jack was badly injured, he tried his best not to show it, but for Mo, being an Apollo, no injury—too small or too big—got past him. Mo rushed to Jack and placed his hands a few centimetres over the injury. He moved them around for a while and bandaged the wound up. Already Jack felt better. Mo pulled him up. Jack stood and was welcomed by five pairs of eyes staring directly at him. He grabbed his bag and began walking away.

'Come on, guys,' he said. 'Let's go kill that Minotaur!'

After a few hours, most of the people had forgotten about what had happened in the morning; Alexa hadn't.

'Psst,' she whispered to Lily. 'Hey, your brother's really dangerous, you know? What if we didn't have a healer with us? What would he have done then? Bled to death? You should tell him to be careful. Anything can happen out here in the wild.'

It had seemed that Jack had heard her.

'Don't worry, Alexa. I'm absolutely fine. Do you see any cuts or bruises?'

'No,' Alexa sighed.

'Exactly, so be quiet and keep walking. We have to get to Tartarus, stop Kronos, and get Mum and Dad back. I haven't seen them for so long I'm beginning to forget what they look like.'

At that moment, he took out a golden-framed photograph of his family, all of them together. He was three, Lily was about seven months, and Mum and Dad were in their early twenties. Jack laughed. He wished they were still beside him. He thought about what would have happened if they were still beside him. Would he even be in this mess?

They kept journeying until they finally left Cendre. They all knew that they would probably already have been in Tartarus walking out with Jack and Lily's parents safe and sound had they used a portal, but according to Zeus, portals attracted monsters, and monsters meant blood.

'Okay, guys,' Lily said. 'Let's stay here for the night.'

That night, they didn't put up the tents and get out their sleeping bags straightaway. Instead, they managed to scrape up all the wood they could find. Since Mo was an Apollo and Apollos had the gift of foresight and clairvoyance, Mo had predicted this would happened, so in his rucksack, he had both marshmallows and wood. The five sat on their rucksacks around the fire, telling each other stories and eating marshmallows.

'Guys, guys,' Leon said, bursting with laughter. 'I've got one. Watch, listen. A mother took her little boy to church. While in church, the little boy said, "Mummy, I have to pee." The mother said to the little boy, "It's not appropriate to say the word *pee* in church. So from now on, whenever you have to pee, just tell me that you have to *whisper*." The following Sunday, the little boy went to church with his father and, during the service, said to his father, "Daddy, I have to whisper." The father looked at him and said, "Okay, just whisper in my ear."'

All of a sudden, bursts of *eurgh*s and *yuck*s jumped from Leon's audience.

'You guys can't take a joke.'

They spent the rest of the night roasting marshmallows and talking about their upcoming battle against one of the strongest mythical creatures around until finally, they became tired.

'Well, guys, I'm going to sleep.' Jack went back into his bed and dreamed.

He dreamt about Zeus talking to him. They talked and talked for hours, and finally, Zeus concluded the conversation with a single sentence: 'The entrance to Tartarus is under the Minotaur's throne.'

CHAPTER 8

It's Just Another Message Written in Blood

'JACK!' Alexa screamed as loudly as she could. She had woken up and found Jack missing from the boys' tent. She had first thought that maybe he was playing a joke on them, but it soon became evident that that wasn't possible. Yet still, inside her, she had hoped that maybe she had been right at first and it was just one of his endless pranks.

Alexa grew to worry more and more as the seconds passed. 'JACK STONE!'

Eventually, she tired and found out it was no use. She knew she would never find him. Well, to be honest, the girl had known that it was no use, but she had just hoped that something might come from trying her best. No matter how hard she tried, there was no way she was going to find him. Today or tomorrow or the day after. She knew she would never find him because she had read the message, the message written in blood. She now knew that the message was most probably written in Jack's blood. She had also been told that there was another message written in blood which had appeared back home at Camp Nikas.

Alexa had never actually been on a quest before. And so this was her first real quest. Despite all the medals and trophies she had hung up over her bed and in her trophy cabinet, she had never been on a quest before. In truth, she was a bit like Annabeth Chase from the Percy Jackson books. Wins all the awards possible, has never been on a quest.

Lily came back out of the woods. 'Any luck?'

Alexa shook her head.

'Mo and Leon haven't found anything either. Oh, Alexa, you should've told us earlier. Why didn't you?'

Lily began to see how upset Alexa really was and hugged her.

'Look, if that Zeus godling Leon Ramirez can't find him—and like I said, he's a Zeus godling—then I'm not expecting an Athena to find him. So there is no need to be upset.'

Lily suddenly realised that she had insulted Athena and quickly intervened by apologising to the goddess of wisdom and battle strategy.

Meanwhile, far away, seconds from Greece, Jack was being chased by an *empusa* and a *lamia*. He had caught them outside writing a message in blood like the one he had read outside the Poseidon cabin. Unfortunately, instead of continuing to read his new book, which he was really getting into, he decided to follow the monsters. Complete and utter idiot. Considering the fact he had recently killed the Nemean Lion, he could probably beat the lamia easily, as it had trouble keeping up with his pace (it had a serpentine tail instead of legs), but the empusa was the tricky bit. When he had first seen them outside the tents, they had hypnotised him with their gaze, but then he remembered the myths. The empusai and lamiae were beautiful beings from the top half of their body, but below, they were hideous creatures. Where their legs should be, the lamiae had the bottom half of any dragon or *drakon*, whereas the empusai, who also had an attractive top half, had one solid leg made of metal and one donkey leg, hence the empusa's great pace. Suddenly, Jack made an abrupt halt. He had reached a dead end. He turned towards the beasts.

'Listen, girls,' he said. 'It doesn't have to be this way. Just let me go, and everything will be fine. Look, let's talk. Why are you even chasing me anyway? I'm just another normal thirteen-year-old whom you found hiding in a tent with a backpack of lethal weapons reading a book. Nothing strange about that, right, girls?'

The couple hissed and, in unison, said (without opening their mouths), 'We have strict orders to write the message and to kill anyone or anything that gets in our way.'

'Girls, look!' Jack pointed towards the sky, and just as he had hoped, the monsters turned. As soon as they had, he lashed out with a front kick, smacking the ball of his foot into . . .

. . . nothing. The creatures were fast and, as a result, had anticipated this trick. Jack knew he was dead and closed his eyes, ready to be taken prisoner by the feared god of death, Thanatos, when all of a sudden, out of nowhere, a centaur galloped out of the forest beside him. He kicked at the floor as if warning them he was about to charge.

'That's what I thought,' he managed through gritted teeth.

The empusa managed to get away; the lamia was not so lucky.

'Jack Stone. I am Diego. You have been expected by my kind. As you can see, I'm a centaur, descendant of the great Pholus, killed by his own tribe. Anyway, may I ask exactly what you are doing here?'

'I don't know, do I? Only a few minutes ago I was reading a *Diary of a Wimpy Kid* book, and now I'm in the middle of a forest stuck with you. No offence.'

Jack took a breath. 'Look, I'm sorry, but you don't understand. I need to get back to my friends. My little sister's there. She's only eleven, she can't look after herself.'

'Where are you guys heading?'

'Crete. We need to get to the Labyrinth.'

Diego stopped for a moment and began to look around him. He was pretty scary for a teenage centaur.

'What's going on?'

'We have to get out of here,' Diego said, nervous. 'Now.'

Night had fallen, and the others still couldn't find Jack. They had decided that tomorrow they would have to split up and begin to do some proper searching. It was no coincidence that the same day Lily lost her brother followed on to the exact night that Lily had a nightmare.

'Jack,' she whispered in her sleep. 'No, no. LEAVE HIM ALONE!'

Suddenly she woke up panting, sweat all over her. Lily didn't usually sweat this bad; in fact, she had hardly ever sweated at all. Lily was a lucid dreamer, meaning she could control her dreams. She forced herself back to sleep, and it worked, but once she was in the dream, somehow she couldn't wake herself up again. Being a lucid dreamer also meant that you could use all your senses during dreams just like in real life. Her dream began like so:

Lily was sitting down on a rock on a lovely summer's day when suddenly a pack of angry wolves came out of nowhere. They snarled at Lily, and the sky began to become dark. One of them pounced on her . . .

It was that short. She woke up for the second time and undid the zip of her and Alexa's tent. She looked out of the tent. It seemed as though the sun had completed its tour for the day and had now been replaced by myriad stars, which dotted the inky canopy. A low waning gibbous moon hovered tenuously in the twilight firmament, bestowing a very dim light upon the land. It was a cool, windy night; the swaying of trees and rustling of leaves could be heard but not seen, as the encompassing darkness had blotted out all but the faintest light. Briefly, a dark, wispy cloud eclipsed the crescent moon. For a few shadowy moments, it looked like there was a halo around the cloud, a dull aura of lunar luminescence.

Orion's Belt could be seen to the north. It had taken its place for the night amongst a thousand other celestial constellations known and unknown, real and imagined. It, too, succumbed to the veil of cloud cover. Patiently, it waited for the nebulous cirrus clouds to pass, waited for the moment it would shine bright once more. Fortunately for Lily, the blood message could still be read. She read it to herself one last time:

Five godlings shall face this threat. Earth or water will face eternal regret. This prophecy must stay concealed or else the sky's secret shall be revealed.

CHAPTER 9

Cool! A Chocolate Milk Dispenser

When Lily woke up, she couldn't believe that the night before, she had had such a bad nightmare. She felt perfect today. Lily had felt that sensational feeling that every footballer must feel after scoring a goal, that every writer must feel after launching a successful new book.

She yawned. 'Good morning, everyone.'

As she began to look around her, she began to notice that she was not in the tent she had gone to sleep in.

'Alexa?' she said.

Suddenly, a figure came out of the darkness and stayed still. He looked as though he had three bodies like that Greek monster Geryon.

'Come here,' he said, staying as still as stone.

Lily just stared at him. She'd been told that an Aphrodite could hypnotise anyone by voice and by staring them directly into the eye. She could never tell Jack, but during his fight with the lion, that was exactly what she did. Though she was scared that he would try to do something like that again while she wasn't there, she couldn't break his heart. She could never.

Apparently, it didn't work on the vague polygon. She got out of her sleeping bag and began to slowly creep up to him until finally she was about five feet away from him. As Lily got closer, she began to realise that he didn't have three bodies; he had one unnaturally, abnormally extra-large-sized body.

'Come closer.'

Lily crept towards him, now trying so hard to hypnotise him that tears began to trickle down her eyes. Then she remembered she could also hypnotise with her voice. As she crept closer to the vague shape, she began to speak.

'When I come to you,' she said, 'you will tell me where my friends are—otherwise your ship will become shipwrecked, literally shipwrecked. I will wreck you and your ship.'

For a moment it was actually working; even though he couldn't be fully hypnotised, he staggered for a moment and his vision became blurry.

'Yes, mistress,' he said, playing along with what he thought was a stupid game.

As soon as Lily was close enough, he backhanded her so hard she landed in a room where she got her head slammed against the wall. She stood up and looked to see if there was a TV control for the TV. Instead, she found all her mates lying on the bed, unconscious. She knew that they'd eventually wake up, so she jumped on to the bed, her head still throbbing with pain, and kept scrolling through the channels until she landed on BBC Breakfast. She looked at her watch. It read six o'clock, meaning it had just started. She had always hated the news and found it extremely boring, so why she stopped on this channel even she had no idea.

'It has been spotted all over Europe, mainly in Greece. Here it is being filmed on a CCTV camera outside a flat in London.'

A massive horned figure, who must've been the 'it', took over the TV screen and began writing a message in blood.

'Here', the news reporter interrupted, 'we have Michael Raven, resident of Reesbury Flat and witness of the incident, informing us about his unfortunate experience.'

She knew that BBC Breakfast usually only reported news like this if it was especially important. Suddenly, Lily turned the TV off. It was because of two simple reasons. One, because she had heard footsteps, and two, because she had heard enough. It had seemed that the son of Minos had been terrorising the whole of Europe, probably with the help of Kronos and 'the sky'.

As the footsteps came closer and closer, Lily began to prepare herself for the dangers that lay ahead. *Bang!*

The door slammed open, and Lily jumped into a ready stance, knowing she might have to defend herself. Then it appeared that Lily didn't have to use her karate at all. A scrawny, thin young boy stood in front of her. He was holding a Nintendo DS in one hand and a plastic cup in the other.

'Here.' He handed the cup to her. 'I'm sorry about what happened earlier with my dad.'

'You should be,' said Lily as she took the glass from him. She took a sip. 'Mm. Delicious. Is that Yazoo?'

'No,' he said, 'but it is chocolate milk. We have a chocolate milk dispenser. Wanna come see?'

Lily followed the boy. He actually didn't look fat or large at all, nothing like his father. In fact, he was really skinny and really tall. He wore an Adidas baseball cap and had crutches, nothing like that large, beefy man. He looked about thirteen, and he also looked as though he could have lost in a fight with a hamster. Across his forehead and other parts of his face, he had a really bad case of acne. The boy took her all the way to the chocolate milk dispenser and got her another cup.

'So what is this place?'

'It's where I live. My mum died when I was little, so it's only me and my dad now. He's the one who sent you here. We saw you guys as we were sailing and decided to help you, so we brought you to the ship. Since you were the only one still asleep, we let you sleep,' he replied.

Lily nodded.

'Aren't you going to say you're sorry that my mum's dead? I mean, that's what most people say.'

'No. My mum *and* dad died, and I know when people say they're sorry, it only makes it worse. They shouldn't feel sorry for you if they don't have anything to do with it.'

'Yeah, I know what you mean.'

'Anyway, what's your name? I'm Lily.'

'Nice name,' the boy said. 'I'm Nick.'

Lily looked around the ship; it looked better than that legendary ship, the *Argo*.

'So a cool ship like this must have a really cool name. What's it called?'

'It's called *Alice's Shadow*. It was named after Mum.'

Lily and Nick stayed up most of the night talking to each other while Nick gave her a tour of the ship. The ship had an endless number of rooms, from the games room to the workroom. Eventually, they reached the subject of species.

'So you're an Aphrodite godling. I'm a satyr.'

'A what?'

'I'm half goat.'

Lily banged her head against the wall, trying to think of something to say that wasn't stupid. It obviously didn't work because all she could say was, 'Uh?'

'Yeah, I get that a lot. Anyway, don't you think it's a bit late for you to be awake? Look, go to bed, and tomorrow, I'll show you our Diet Pepsi dispenser.'

'I would've preferred Fanta, but I guess Diet Pepsi's okay. See you tomorrow,' said Lily.

'Bye,' said Nick.

The next morning, Lily woke up alone and began to look for her friends. She went downstairs, still in her pyjamas, and found the other godlings there surrounding a cylindrical shape with a face on it. As she came closer to the object, she began to realise that the face looked familiar. Very familiar.

'Jack. Yep, that's definitely Jack,' the girl muttered. Lily was filled with rage and fury. How could he do this to her? He had promised that the team would stick together and that they'd get through this quest safely, and by the time they had finished, everything would be back to normal. Now he had broken his promise as, my reader, he does in many parts of this story, particularly towards the ending.

Lily had even made a list of what she would do when she got her hands on Jack, and of course, she had titled it exactly that.

What to do when I get my hands on Jack:

1. Use a lethal back kick on his fat face.
2. Tell him I hate him.
3. Get Nick to take off his baseball cap and smash his horns into Jack's chest.
4. Pour all the chocolate milk from the dispenser on his head.
5. Make sure he doesn't forget my revenge!

She pushed everyone out of the way until she stood face-to-face with her thirteen-year-old brother.

She grabbed the cylindrical communicator and began, 'Jack Stone! You had better have a good explanation for why you, young man, were not in the tent when we all woke up!'

It seemed to go on for hours, but now everyone knew why Jack hadn't been with the boys in their tents when they woke up. Lily couldn't wait to meet her brother in Greece; however, she hadn't forgotten her special punishments.

After speaking to Jack, Lily decided she was going to spend the rest of the day on her own in the games room. The games room was her favourite room in *Alice's Shadow* because it had Wi-Fi and she could keep in touch with her other friends. She took out her iPhone and went straight on to Skype. She and her friends talked for hours and hours. She had told them that she'd gone back to Australia with Jack. They believed her mainly because she and Jack always went to Australia on the holidays even though Jack never wanted anyone to know he was Australian.

After that, Lily felt bored. 6L's teacher, Mr Lau, had set them some holiday homework. All it was, was some extra SATs papers. Despite Lily being the smartest in her class, even she found them difficult. She grabbed her school bag, opened it up, and began to rummage through it until she found the science test. Lily wrote her name and surname and the date. She began the test.

'Question 1.' Lily looked at her paper. 'Seriously?'

The question had asked if two north poles on separate magnets were to face each other, would they attract or repel. The question was a two-mark question, and Lily explained that they would repel and why. In a few seconds, she had finished the first page.

After finishing the test, Lily left the games room feeling happy. She was no longer worried about her SATs. After that test, she knew it was going to be a walk in a park, but still, she didn't want to get to arrogant.

Lily went to the kitchen. She looked around and realised no one was there. She sat by the kitchen table and began to think. She couldn't believe what she had signed up for. In five days, they would be out in an ancient maze constructed by an ancient demigod, ready to fight. She didn't know if she could handle that. Finding out your parents' killer is on the loose was one thing, but fighting for your life against the Minotaur to avenge their life is a whole other. She recited the prophecy that was graphitised outside the tents: 'Five godlings shall face this threat, earth or water will face eternal regret, this prophecy must stay concealed or else the sky's secret shall be revealed.' Lily repeated the prophecy three times, and on the third time, she stopped after the first line.

'Earth?' she said to herself. 'Well, my surname is Stone, but what about the water part?'

She strained her brain so hard to think.

'Wait, Alexa's surname is Rivera. River. Rivers have water. The sky. Who is the sky? Wait, what if. . . no, it can't be.'

Lily dropped her cup of chocolate milk on to the floor.

'Capital *S—sky*? In Greek mythology, the sky god, the *actual* sky, was. . . Ouranos.'

CHAPTER 10

Uninvited Guests

Lily had figured out the prophecy and didn't like the outcome. She didn't have any idea of how she was going to tell the others. It didn't make any sense. Kronos had killed his father, Ouranos, and now they were working together? She didn't understand this at all. She knew something horrible was going to happen.

'That's it,' she said to herself; she had had enough of this. 'C'mon, Lily. Breathe in and out.'

She couldn't do anything. Fear had overcome her. She just stood there as a statue, like a monument frozen for eternity. The fear she felt was a being in itself because it wasn't just in her; it was all around her.

She crept out of the kitchen, gobsmacked. Suddenly. . .

'Get out,' Nick's father rasped. 'You don't belong here. None of you do!'

He grabbed Lily and threw her all the way across the room. There was nothing Lily could do. He reached into his right pocket and pulled out a gun. The gun was a Baby Eagle II BE9915R. It was a 9 mm pistol, and Lily knew that one twitch of his finger would send a 9 mm bullet shattering through her skull and into her brain. She was scared. Of course, any normal human being would be. Lily looked around; there had to be some way of escape. Still, there was nothing she could do. She had to do something and quick, otherwise. . . No, Lily wasn't going to let that happen. She'd have to get through him the old-fashioned way. Distract, strike, and run. Reluctantly, she stood. She opened her mouth to speak but was interrupted when Nick shot the chandelier above her. *Crash!* It fell to the ground, but Lily just managed to dodge it.

'I'm not afraid to use it,' he said. 'Even against a little girl like you!'

Lily swore under her breath. That had been her original plan—to look young and innocent, to get him to think, *What am I doing? I can't shoot a little girl.*

Now she would have to improvise. She knew her way out: the nearby window. But she would have to be careful; if she timed the jump wrong, she would fall into the sea and drown.

'Look, Mr—?' Lily just realised that she didn't even know the sailors' family name.

'Kent, Mike Kent,' he said, still pointing the gun.

'Look, Mr Kent. Why are you even doing this? What have I done to you?'

Lily checked how far the window was. She was making progress. The window was almost directly behind her. Almost. From now on she would have to be careful; her next six steps were the most dangerous. She breathed in and out and got ready. She crept a few more steps, her hands held up high.

Now she had to get him to shoot the gun. *Think, Lily, think. What shall I say?* Lily's plan was to get him to shoot the gun at the window's handle and jump out. Opening it herself was a good way to get shot. So she did the first thing that came to her mind: Alice Kent.

'I bet that loser wife of yours Alice was it? wouldn't be as cruel as you. Actually, I think she was probably just as a psychopath as you are. I mean, what kind of an idiot would marry someone as ugly as you,' Lily said.

She had planned to go on, but she didn't need to. *Bang!* The bullet smashed right through the handle. Lily didn't even have to dodge. She elbowed the glass, sending shards going everywhere. All she had to do now was jump out; in Lily's opinion, it was not as easy as it sounded. Millions of bullets exploded millimetres above her head. She blew him a brief kiss and jumped back, with her legs finishing off the already smashed window. Suddenly, looking down at the deep blue sea, young Lily didn't feel so confident. She had never been a good swimmer, and if she timed her next step wrong, she knew there was no coming back. There was no 'There'll always be tomorrow.' If she failed, she was dead. Lily closed her eyes and breathed in then out. In then out. In, out. She looked back down then back up from where she had fallen. She was nearly there. One. . . two. . . three. . . She grabbed on to the guttering and began to shimmy across, her legs submerged in the ice-cold water below. With all the strength she managed to gather, she flipped forward, smacking the heel of her shoes into the window on the first floor of the ship and climbed in. She was there. . . but so was someone else: Kent. The gun had one last bullet, and Lily knew where it was going. *Smack!* The bullet ripped through the air, flying across the little space between them and straight through her forehead . . .

Lily woke up and sat bolt upright, like she had just been shot by lightning, panting. What seemed like gallons of sweat cascaded down her face. It was just a dream. A nightmare. She looked around. Alexa slept next to her. Everything stayed silent.

'Can't sleep?' asked a familiar voice coming from the edge of the bed. At once, Lily realised it was Alexa. She'd recognise that voice anywhere. Suddenly, she felt the urge to tell her all about her dream, and so she did—well, all except for the discovery of the meaning of the prophecy. She didn't want to worry her yet.

'So how come *you* can't sleep?' Lily asked.

'It's just I'm worried about Jack. I know that he's in the hands of a centaur, but I just can't bear the thought of losing him again.'

'Well,' said Lily, 'take it from his big sister: Jack. Can. Look after. Himself. So stop worrying, and get some sleep. We have a big day tomorrow.'

Alexa took Lily's advice and fell asleep as soon as her head hit the pillow. On the other hand, it wasn't the same story with Lily. Something was making a clicking noise. It was coming from the room next to hers. Mr Kent's room. Lily jumped out of bed, not bothering to change her clothes, and crouched down. She began to tiptoe across the corridor separating the two rooms. There was noise, like someone was talking. Lily didn't manage to make out much, but what she did manage to get didn't make much sense.

'The Stone girl . . .'

'He's coming . . .'

'Two o'clock tomorrow . . .'

Lily looked at her watch. It was 3.26. Someone was coming at two o'clock tomorrow. But why had they mentioned her? Today was the day they were going to see Jack. Lily looked through the keyhole. Mr Kent stood opposite a figure. An ugly figure. It looked about ten feet tall with a bulky neck. He looked about the same size as Zeus. Lily knew at once that that was the Minotaur. But what was he doing with Kent? And why was he allowed on *Alice's Shadow?* Lily knew the answer at once: he was working with Kent. All of a sudden, Lily heard footsteps coming towards the door. *Thump. Thump. Thump.* Lily began to scuttle away like an unwanted insect towards her room. *Clang!*

'Ouch!' Lily whisper-shouted.

She turned. Her right foot had hit a cold piece of metal. Her ankle was throbbing with pain.

She looked at her watch again: 3.29. Lily knew she wasn't going to get any sleep even if she stole Mo's blanket, so for that exact reason, Lily crawled like a baby to the vent and tried to force it open. It didn't work; the vent was screwed on to tight.

'Okay,' she said, 'Be like that.'

Lily took a breath and placed her two hands on the left side of the vent. One. . . two. . . three. . . pull. One. . . two. . . three. . . pull. She breathed.

'One last time.' She managed this, her back aching.

Suddenly, she felt the vent become loose. Slowly, she pulled it to the side, making sure nobody heard. She climbed in, her ankle still throbbing. Lily was thinking about how exactly she was going to get back to bed when she heard footsteps, the exact same footsteps she had heard when Kent and his 'boss' had been walking towards the door.

'Lily?'

A cold hand fell upon her shoulder. Lily turned expeditiously. In front of her was, sat on his knees, a boy of about thirteen years of age. He had a scar running from his right eye to his left lower cheek. His long blond hair was as wild as the jungle, untamable and a danger to the comb. Lily gawped at his electric-blue eyes.

'Jack? What are *you* doing here?'

'Well, hello to you too. Typical. I travel half the world to find you, and all I get is a "What are you doing here?"'

'Shut up. I'm kinda busy here.'

'Doing what exactly?'

Lily took a deep breath and said, without taking a single breath, 'I've just jumped out of bed, forgotten to get dressed, crept down to some weird locked room, listened to Mr Kent talk to some weirdo for five minutes, sprained my ankle, pulled open a vent, crept in only to find this *thing*,'—she gestured to Jack—'and. . . Well, yeah, that's pretty much it.'

'Cool. Just like to point out you never answered my question.'

Lily gave her older brother her 'I'm about to kill you' look and screamed, 'Shut up!'

Her voice echoed and somersaulted over and over again in the claustrophobic amount of space that was their hideout. Lily was certain that it had escaped into a new proximity, possibly Mr. Kent's. And then Lily's concern was confirmed.

'Hear that, boss?'

'What?'

'We've some uninvited guests. The Stone girl.' Peter Kent gritted his teeth.

'Well, Kent, you know the drill. I want her dead.'

CHAPTER 11

A Mother's Intuition

'Lily, where are you? Come on. This is getting boring. I'm *fourteen*. I am *not* going to play hide-and-seek.'

It had been fifteen minutes now. Wherever Alexa looked, Lily was not there.

'Oi! Mo, get up,' Alexa scolded, 'and you too, Leon!'

'But . . . but what about the winner of the best bicep contest? It's so gonna be me. I'm in the finals!'

Mo sat up on his bed, his elbows pressing down against his whispery pillow. 'Leon, Leon, Leon,' he sighed, 'You will never win anything to do with any form of exercise or fitness. You can't even run five metres without falling to the ground panting and crying for help.'

'Whatever. And anyway, you can't even swim.'

'Just like to add—neither can you.'

'But my front crawl's beautiful. My swimming teacher said I looked like a monkey leaping gracefully through the trees.'

Mo fell off his bed, laughing.

Alexa couldn't believe what she was witnessing: two godlings arguing about monkeys and backstrokes.

She had to step in. 'Pack it in! We have to find Lily and quick before something happens. Something bad.'

Leon grabbed a Manchester United top from his wardrobe and put it over his jumper. Mo took off his trousers (after forcing everyone to face the wall) and put on his favourite pair of jeans. Alexa didn't bother to get changed; she didn't need to. It was just a trip to the bottom of the stairs and then back up again.

'Okay, guys,' she whispered. 'We're gonna go downstairs, find Lily, and get her upstairs.' Suddenly, Alexa began to mumble, 'Something like that dream of hers.'

'Sorry, Alexa?' Mo asked.

'Um, nothing.'

'For goodness' sake, would you please stop?' exclaimed an irritated Lily Stone. It had been the fifth time Jack had smacked his fingers across her back.

'Stop what?' he laughed.

'Stop breathing and living!'

Jack wasn't really offended, and to be honest, he didn't really care. He was used to being insulted and cussed at by his younger sister. After all, in his perspective, she was just a spoilt little attention seeker. But he still loved her more than anything in the world.

Suddenly, Lily heard footsteps. Large, heavy footsteps smacking at the wooden floor. Who was it? What was it?

'Shush,' she whispered to Jack. 'I can hear something. Something big.'

Instantly, they headed for the opening of the vent, ready to leap out, but it was too late. *Smack!* Jack fell back to the ground on his shoulder. Something was wrong. Non-hesitantly, he jumped back up into the *renoji-dachi* stance, ready for anything. He scanned the room until finally his eyes landed on a target. He lashed out with the ball of his foot, using one of the most lethal karate kicks. *Yoko-geri,* the side kick. His Nikes made contact with his opponent's upper chest, and he heard the voice of a male. He looked down at the recipient of the kick. It was someone he had not been expecting. Someone he could have called a friend. Mo Lawson.

'Ow, what was that for?'

Jack jumped down to Mo's level and placed his hand over his mouth.

'Shush!'

There was silence for about thirty seconds. Then Jack heard the unmistakeable sound of a *fukibari* being shot. A fukibari was a small, dangerous needle concealed in the mouths of ninjas. Experts could shoot up to twelve of them at the same time.

The fukibari soared through the air and into Jack's neck. The needle contained a sleeping drug which knocked him out instantly. His vision became a sudden blur, and all he could hear was the screaming of a woman. Despite the fact she was screaming, her voice was as gentle as ever. She sounded like his little sister, Lily. The screaming stopped. Suddenly, two distant figures materialised. A male and a female. He had seen them before. Where? He had no idea. Pictures, perhaps. Maybe videos. The male had close-cropped brown hair and was wearing a suit. The female looked very familiar, as did the man, and had long blond hair that fell gracefully around her shoulders. She was wearing a long white coat that looked like something Jack would wear in chemistry back at school. She waved at Jack.

'Bye, Jack,' she whispered.

The male looked at him, his dark eyes boring into the teenager.

'Bye, son.'

Jack Stone woke up almost three hours later. He was in pain. That's all he knew. His head was throbbing, his heart pounding, and he felt like someone (or something) had managed to tie a knot in his neck. It was a feeling Jack knew all too well. He had been knocked out before by Edward Sterling during break time in Year 7 by the senior black belts in his karate class and by the local gang NM (no mercy). And it was no different this time. The slow climb back to the world of air and light.

The first thing that hit him was the smell. Even before Jack opened his eyes, he knew where he was. The tantalizing scent of washed-up waves and bananas all rolled into one. Jack could feel the millions of grains of sand hot against his fingers and the cool breeze against his face—a relief from the sweltering sun.

He heard the sea crawling onto the sand and, further away, the same monster dashing against the rocks. As he opened his mouth to take in a gulp of air, he tasted salt in his throat. Not the same taste as on Brighton Pier when you look over into the sea, but a fresh, clean one, as if taking in pure oxygen. Only then, when Jack's four other senses had taken in their share of his surroundings, did he allow himself to open his eyes. He was amazed at how easily fantasy and reality intertwined at that moment. For Jack, it was like continuing a dream after waking up.

As he lifted his eyelids, as the barrier between Jack's imagination and actuality was removed, the accuracy of his prediction astounded him.

But where were the others? None of them could be seen.

Jack managed to stand up. He crept towards the sea and put his foot in the water. It was warm. He turned around and stared at the large canopy of trees a few meters away from him.

Laughter. He could hear laughter. But how? He was on his own, wasn't he? He began towards the forest, growing more and more nervous with every step he took. What if the forest was home to tigers? Or maybe more lions? He remembered what had happened with the Nemean lion he had fought last time. A massive cut across his forearm. Mo had fixed it last time, but now Mo wasn't here.

'Hello? Is there anyone there?'

No answer.

Jack had no choice but to continue forward. He could feel an aura of power around him, probably coming from the water. He was a Poseidon godling after all.

He turned to face the sea.

CHAPTER 12

Crete

Daniel and Tamara Stone knew that there was no way out of this. There hadn't been for ten years. They had never believed Kronos when he had told them that Jack and Lily were still looking for them, but now they had seen it themselves.

'At least they're away from Alistair and Mary,' reassured Tamara.

'I know. Instead, they're in the hands of Kronos *and* under the watchful eye of Ouranos!'

Daniel placed his heavy head in his palms. Suddenly, he felt a jolt of pain that ran through his body. Then he remembered. He had used his shirt as a bandage over his bicep after cutting himself on a shard of glass a few days ago. Or a few weeks ago? Maybe even more. It was hard to keep track of time in Tartarus, almost impossible to be honest. Tamara went up to her husband. She placed her arm around his shoulders and tried to comfort him. Of course, it didn't work.

'Look, it's not your fault. Was it you who sent the Nemean lion after them? Was it?'

Reluctantly, Mr Stone replied, 'No.'

'Exactly. We just have to stay strong until something happens.'

Tamara knew inside that no matter what happened, there was no way she could fix anything. No matter how hard she tried, they wouldn't be able to get out of Tartarus. Daniel reached into his back pocket and reached for his phone. He knew it was pointless as there was no signal in Tartarus, but it reminded him of his son. He had a Chelsea phone case which Jack had forced him to buy when he was three. The same year that Jack had been sent into care. He had taught Jack karate from a very early age and decided it would be best to send him to proper classes. Daniel hoped he still attended regularly.

He remembered how good his old life was. Jack was doing well at school, Tamara had recently given birth to Lily, he had just signed a five-year contract with Chelsea, and then inevitably, Kronos had got him abducted and brought him to this dump. He remembered it like it was yesterday. (For all Daniel knew, it could've been. Like I said, it was hard to keep track of time in Tartarus.) He and Tamara had just driven the kids back home after the match. Jack, his wife, and him were cheering after the 4–0 match against Liverpool. Daniel had scored a hat-trick and had assisted the famous left-winger, Adam Michaels. Even his seven-month-old daughter seemed to have managed a tiny smile across her face. So far so good, but soon—and Daniel knew it was unavoidable—something, something no supervillain could ever imagine, was about to go very wrong.

The time was about half past four on that very crestfallen Saturday. To celebrate Chelsea's victory, the Stones had, immediately after the game, stopped at the nearest McDonald's. Daniel had ordered for everyone, getting a Happy Meal for Jack and two wraps for him and his wife. They had decided that Lily was too young and could possibly choke on the rock-hard chips, so instead, she had to settle for her milk bottle. Tamara had put Jack to sleep early as he had a birthday party to attend tomorrow morning. As Tamara was leaving Jack's brightly coloured bedroom, she heard downstairs what sounded like her husband groaning in pain. Quickly, she rushed downstairs.

'Danny!' Tamara had screamed, growing more and more worried by the second.

She had managed to get down to the living room, when suddenly she had found, sprawled across the floor, a body. The body of Daniel Stone.

She got down on her knees, placing her hand across his chest. He was badly bruised, and blood trickled from his forehead down to his cheek. Without warning, she was grabbed by the shoulder and thrown from one side of the room to the other. She began to crawl backwards without taking her eyes off the figure. He had cold dark features and a nose that looked like it had been broken one too many times. She got up and lashed out with her right elbow. The man was fast. He jumped back and grabbed her wrist. Using his free hand, he backhanded her, immediately knocking her out.

That was the one thing she was sure of. She was unconscious.

Jack discovered that the laughter was coming from Lily and the others. He was glad that he had managed to find them. He wasn't so glad that they were laughing at him. He tackled his sister with a hug as soon as he found them.

Alexa had immediately known that the island they were stuck on was Crete.

Jack wasn't so sure. 'How do you know we're in Crete? For all we know, this could be Mauritius.'

'It's Crete. I know for sure that we are currently standing on Cretan soil.'

Jack reached for his bag. He took out a packet of Walker's Cheese and Onion Crisps.

'So', he began, crisps leaping out of his mouth, 'if this really is Crete, then we need to get to the Labyrinth to defeat the Minotaur, right?'

'Well, duh!'

Jack thought about this for a while. He was on his way to the Labyrinth, right? And Zeus had mentioned that the entrance to Tartarus was directly under the Minotaur's throne. His mum and dad were in Tartarus. What if he could kill two birds with one stone? What if he could save his mum and dad and kill the Minotaur? He could help save the world and help himself, but he would be risking the lives of Leon, Mo, Alexa, and most importantly, his little sister. Could he take that risk? And how would he be able to cope if (the Greek gods forbid) something went wrong? He would never be able to live it down, yet if it all went well, he would finally be happy. Jack would have to think about this more carefully, but for now, he decided to go to sleep.

Jack Stone couldn't stop smiling. He was going to save his mum and dad. They were going to live together as a family. He could have friends over for visits (the Sterlings didn't allow visits from any of Jack or Lily's friends). Jack could finally live life as a normal thirteen-year-old boy. He walked up to the sea and dived in.

Leaping downwards through air, Jack immersed himself in the element that felt to him like soft velvet. Gliding through its luxurious depths, feeling one with his oceanic universe, he could feel his strength and immortality. Breath flew into and through Jack's body, giving his arms and legs the power to stroke and kick as he watched the mystical light playing amid the undulating currents in silvery whites, blues, and rainbow colours. Time stood still as the child's body moved silently and serenely, joyfully.

Finally, he crept out of the sea and began to swim back to the shore.

'C'mon, Jack,' Leon called. 'We need to get going.'

And so their most terrifying journey yet had begun.

CHAPTER 13

Lily Knocks Out a Famous, Extremely Muscular Greek Bandit

'I'm tired.' Leon sighed, slumping against a nearby boulder. 'I don't wanna carry on!'

'Leon, we're all tired.' Jack reached into his Chelsea backpack and pulled out a bottle of Coke. 'Here, have this, might wake you up a bit.'

He threw it in Leon's direction and kept walking.

They had been walking for ages, but so far they hadn't come across any trouble—a good sign.

Jack couldn't wait until the day he would finally manage to save his mother and father. When would that day come? Well, that was one thing he was unsure about. He had packed some books with him just in case he got bored. Jack loved reading and had about half a dozen hardbacks stored in his bag, but he had only managed to fit in two throughout his whole journey: *Lord of the Flies* by William Golding and *Diary of a Wimpy Kid: Old School*. Jack wished that he could reach out for another novel, sit down, and begin to read until the cows came home; however, in a situation like this, he knew that that wish would never become true.

Lily sensed something was wrong with her brother. She could see it in his eyes. It was as if someone very close to him had recently fallen to their death.

'Jack, you okay?' She remembered how only a few days ago she had asked the exact same question while the siblings were sprawled across their bed.

'I'm cool'.

Suddenly the sadness and emptiness she had sensed microseconds ago turned into rainbows, gaiety and joy. Lily remembered how euphoric he had looked when he had got a role in the school production of *Grease*. She had thought that that was the happiest he would ever get; she was wrong. This was.

Although Lily was missing all her friends back at Beachwood, she knew she wouldn't be able to cope with the separation of the godlings. But at the same time, she knew that they had to. The longer they stayed together, the higher the chance they would get killed. And if they got killed, millions of others would too. Suddenly, jumping out of nowhere was what seemed to be the five's next enemy. The bandit stood tall at seven feet. He was slightly smaller than a gypsy caravan, his face ugly and swollen. His arms rippled with muscles, but his legs were a whole other story. They looked small and crippled. Anyone could've easily described them as 'twisted'.

Almost immediately, Alexa realised the true identity of the crippled man. 'I know you! You're . . . you're Periphetes!'

Mo looked puzzled. 'Pair-of-Feeties? Who on Olympus is that?'

Periphetes ignored the boy. 'My legend precedes me! If you know the wondrous word that is my name, surely you must know that it is pointless to try to negotiate!'

Jack didn't need an explanation. The heads strewn around the soft undergrowth of the forest were enough. Cautiously, he backed away.

'You see these heads?' He pointed to the area where, only a few seconds ago, Jack had his eyes fixed. 'I pound them to the ground with this almighty club!'

He showed the godlings a large bronze club, which was surrounded by intricate carvings, some large, some small.

He smacked it down the palm of his hands a few times to show off. 'Solid oak core covered in twenty sheets of bronze.'

Only now had it struck the campers how heavy the club actually was.

Out of the five, Leon was the most bewildered. '*Twenty* sheets of bronze? Come on, mate. That would make it too heavy for anyone to carry.'

Periphetes smirked an evil smirk. 'I am strong. It has the power to kill any grown man, no matter how strong they are. Like I said, it would be pointless to try anything funny.'

'So', Lily replied, 'can we get past?'

'You make me laugh, child. I will rob you, then I will kill you!'

Lily had planned for this to happen. She remembered the trick that Jade had taught her. She smiled. 'You *will* let us pass. You *will* hand over the club.' Lily could see that already the fugitive was getting weak and extremely dizzy.

'Yes, master. Yes, Aphrodite.' The bandit stood aside and let the girl pass after handing over his precious club.

Just as Jack and the others were about to follow Lily, he escaped his trance and stood back in his original position.

'Only the girl passes.' Periphetes cracked his knuckles and opened his mouth to speak. Nothing came out. Lily had lashed out with the back of her hand, driving it into the man's temple.

'I believe we have a monster we need to beat up. Let's get going.'

For the rest of the journey, everyone was quiet. After witnessing the strongest man in the world getting knocked out—perhaps even falling to his death—by this eleven-year-old girl, nobody wanted to get on the wrong side of her. Jack knew this best. Once, when Lily was still in Year 1, he had seen her headbutt another girl for handing over Lily's school bag. After watching the girl cry for about ninety seconds, she said, 'I can get my own bag, thank you very much!'

Ever since then, Jack had been very careful around his sister. He didn't want to spend a week in hospital.

Ouranos sat there, staring at the *ider*. How could this have happened? The kids were tantalizingly close to the Labyrinth. If they reached their destination in time, then . . . then. The primordial god couldn't bear to think about the outcome if they completed their quest. Ouranos's goal was to take revenge on all those who had forgotten him. Over thousands of years ago, Kronos's mother had forced him to kill Ouranos. He had told his father of this news, and the two had come up with a plan. On the night of the murder, Kronos would never really bring down the scythe across his father. Instead, Ouranos had got a mere mortal to take his place. He had used simple magic to make the human appear like him. His son had spared his life; however, if their plan, Project X, failed, Ouranos wouldn't spare his. He had concocted the ider himself. This was slightly more complicated magic, but the god had executed it, once again, brilliantly. An ider was like a crystal ball. It showed you the exact location of the person—or people—you were looking for. The five had shocked him. They were puny teenagers, two of them only eleven, yet they had made more progress than any adult could. How this was possible, he had no idea. But one thing was for sure: they were was no way he was going to let them leave alive.

CHAPTER 14

The Labyrinth

Leon couldn't believe his eyes. There it stood in front of him, tall and elegant. Despite the fact that it had been sitting there ever since the time of King Minos of Crete, it looked magnificent. He couldn't believe that in only a few hours' time, he and the rest of the campers would be risking the life of such a monument. Leon knew an amazing building or sculpture when he saw one. It was because of his passion for architecture that he was often mistaken as a Hephaestus godling. Leon knew that Daedalus was a remarkable inventor (of course he had heard stories back at Camp Nikas), but only now had he actually seen a piece of his work.

The others were equally astonished. Lily had grabbed her iPhone and couldn't stop taking pictures.

From far away, it was almost impossible to tell that it hosted a brutal, lethal weapon that was the Minotaur.

Jack, Lily, Alexa, Leon, and Mo all knew that at some point that day, they would have to kill the Minotaur.

Jack hadn't told the others about his plan to rescue Daniel and Tamara Stone. They would have just worried about him and consequently told him to forget about it. He had to save his parents. Without them, he was miserable. Without them, he would forever be known as the Boy Whose Parents Just Don't Care or the Boy Who Has No One. He wasn't going to let that happen. No matter what or who came in his way, he was going to get his parents back, and this time, he couldn't care less about what anyone had to say. But first, before he saved his parents, he was going to have to defeat the Minotaur.

'Come on, guys. We have a bull to beat.'

After hours of walking, they came to an abrupt halt. They were stood exactly outside the Labyrinth. Everybody except Jack was trembling with fear. Jack couldn't afford being scared. After all, he was about to save his parents.

The giant stone goats rolled open as if they were automatic. The five hadn't expected this to be so easy. They had probably expected more security. But then again, it wasn't like anyone could steal anything with the Minotaur in there.

Jack yelled, 'Yeah, Labyrinth! Woohoo!'

He ran in the direction of the open gates; the others' eyes fixed upon him, staring quizzically. The rest of the four followed, not quite as enthusiastically. Suddenly, the gates slammed shut.

They headed into the maze.

The place had been designed to be confusing. After four or five steps, everyone was hopelessly lost. They made their way past the best archers in Crete, terrifying swordsmen, and snakes that probably contained enough venom to take out a London comprehensive. Finally, the Labyrinth opened into what looked like a distant cousin of the Coliseum.

Waiting for them—the Minotaur. He'd managed to grow to the unnatural height of eight feet tall. And with his bullish shoulders, peculiarly large neck, and his blood-red eyes and dagger-like horns, he could make any creature jump out of its skin. His limbs were swollen with muscles. He wore only a loincloth, which was stained with blood and dirt. All around him, the floor was strewn with bones, broken limbs, and parts of skeletons. Other than that was a pile of old hay, a well to drink from, and an old hole dug ages ago for a toilet. He could understand why the Minotaur was angry.

Mo didn't know if to feel petrified, intrigued, or just sorry for the monster. After all, it wasn't its fault that it had to live in such a dump.

Without hesitation, the beast charged. If anyone had felt any sympathy for the Minotaur in the last few moments, it all changed now. He'd been taught since birth to kill, to hate, to show no emotion. Alexa dived out of the way. She was too slow. The Minotaur had lost enormous amounts of blood, and it seemed that it wasn't going to stop there. It kept on running towards Alexa.

'Noooo!' Jack threw himself across the arena and grabbed on to the Minotaur's horns. He pulled them back as viciously as he could. He fell back and landed on the hay. Suddenly, he realised that the monstrosity was falling with him. Surely the bull man's weight would kill him. Jack had microseconds to get out of the way; that was exactly what he did.

Slam! The Minotaur landed, and the impact of the fall threw Jack against the wall. Meanwhile, Lily and Mo had crept behind the animal, wrapping some old string they found (probably left from the Greek hero Theseus) around his horns. Involuntarily, the Minotaur jumped up. The friends yanked with all their strength until they finally heard the satisfying snapping sound they were hoping for. Both horns had broken off at their bases.

The Minotaur howled in pain, 'Aaargghhh!'

He got up, ignoring the searing pain that was dancing around his head. He balled his fist as his eyes bore into the children. He had been warned about them, but there wasn't any chance that he was going to let himself be beaten by a group of teens. He charged, this time losing all sense of self-control. But for once, the teens had anticipated his move. Jack lashed out with a side kick, slamming the ball of his foot into the creature's solar plexus. He stumbled, got up, and decided to carry on, not knowing that in a few seconds, he would be regretting that decision. Alexa dragged her sword across its chest, drawing blood, while simultaneously, Leon reached into Mo's backpack and fired three arrows into the Minotaur's back. It growled in response and backhanded the boy so that he landed over the skeletons, but still it carried on. Lily and Mo stabbed the horns into his chest. It staggered, muttering Greek curses, and then finally fell to its death.

It tried to move, but the movement only made the pain worse. At last, the hybrid creature closed its eyes, and its thousand-year journey of life finally came to an end.

It was only now that Jack realised the large golden throne was the throne of the Minotaur. Supposedly, the entrance to Tartarus was directly underneath it. He had made the decision, and now he was going to stick by it.

That he knew.

He dashed towards his sister and leaped at her with a hug. 'I'll be back, Lily. I'll be back.'

He grabbed his bag and slung it over his shoulder as he began to run towards the throne. He fell to the floor and rolled and rolled until he reached what looked like a trapdoor. Quickly, he opened it.

By the time Lily realised what her brother was doing, it was too late. He had already entered Tartarus.

CHAPTER 15

Into Tartarus

Already, Jack had lost track of how long he had been falling—minutes? hours? days? It felt like an eternity. His foot was searing with pain from when he had kicked the Minotaur. It felt like kicking a solid wall. He didn't want to meet the creature again at the bottom. Of course, that was assuming there even *was* a bottom. Hopefully he wouldn't be flattened on impact. A few seconds later, the whistling in his ears became more of a roar as the air became intolerably hot, permeated with an unpleasant stench.

Crash!

Jack had crashed against the ground, and fortunately, the impact didn't kill him. He was surrounded by burning fires and erupting volcanoes. Tartarus was massive. He might never even find his mum and dad. It would definitely be a miracle if he did.

'Mum! Dad! It's your son, Jack.'

Jack kept trying and trying; it was no use. He kept on walking until he found a large rock. He sat on it and began to sob like there was no tomorrow. He sobbed and sobbed. He even swore at himself. He spat out a single foul, ugly word.

And then he looked up.

There in the distance stood two dark figures, vaguely humanoid, running towards him. At first he thought it was Kronos and Ouranos. But as the polygons got closer, he began to make out a female figure with blond hair and a round, boyish face and a muscular-looking man wearing a bandage over his arm.

'Mum and Dad,' he murmured while suddenly getting louder. 'Mum and Dad!'

A massive smile ran across his face from one ear to the other.

The three of them all jumped at each other.

Daniel was the first to get up, and as soon as he did, he grabbed his son's wrist and pulled him up.

'Oh, Jack. You don't know how happy I am to see you!'

'No, Dad. *You* don't know how happy *I* am to see you!'

Suddenly, euphoria became worry.

Thud! Thud! Thud!

They could hear footsteps slamming down rapidly on the hard floor, as if someone was running.

'AARGH!' The voice came out of nowhere. 'You will not get away!'

Jack seized on to both his parents' hands, and the trio began to run. To Jack's surprise, his parents were a lot faster than he had actually thought. Another advantage. Finally, they had reached the place that Jack had started at.

Tamara squeezed her son tight. 'When I say *go*. One, two, three, *go!*'

The three jumped up simultaneously and managed to kick the trapdoor open. They were through. But so were their pursuers. They didn't want to die. Consequently, they ran towards the other four.

'Quick, Leon. Use your magic!'

Leon had no idea what was going on, but he was not one to disobey.

'*Mayotara!*'

As if it were a contagious disease, starting with Leon, everyone closed their mouth and held their breath. Each and every one of them vanished in turn.

Suddenly, a massive cloud surrounded them as if they were flying high in the sky.

Kronos and Ouranos couldn't believe their eyes. In front of them lay the dead carcass of the Minotaur. Blood poured out of two holes punctured into his chest. They really had lost to a group of children.

Ouranos felt something burning white hot inside him. It was anger. How could this stupid man fail to defeat five children? It was like molten lava flowing through his intestines. He looked down deliberately, knowing he would be unable to keep the emotion out of his eyes. He would have to deal with his son in his own time, but for now, he would need to hire someone, perhaps an assassin, to get rid of the kids. He had learnt his lesson. Project X had failed despite the amount of time, effort, and money he had put into it. He had learnt that these children were unnaturally good and had defeated the great Kronos and escaped the dark wrath of Ouranos. He thought back to the idea of using an assassin to finish the children off, but the person he had in mind had every reason to refuse, every reason to ignore his request.

My reader, I apologise for not pulling you aside to talk to you for a long time; however, it was all leading up to this very moment. I am sure you are dying to know all about this assassin. If so, I will now continue. I would also like to add something else. If you remember, one of our heroes was sat outside a door overhearing some people talking. Someone was supposed to come at two 'o clock. Am I right? As you have noticed, I have mentioned no more about the delivery for that will have to be discussed in a whole other story. Anyway, back to subjects with greater significance.

The person Ouranos had been thinking of was the woman who had intricately planned his own death and had come very close to succeeding. Yes, the person he had been thinking of was Gaia, the bride of Ouranos.

CHAPTER 16
Back Home

Daniel and Tamara were ecstatic; finally, they were reunited with their children. Leon had originally magically transported them to Camp Nikas. While their parents talked to Zeus and signed official paperwork, Jack and Lily had a chance to say goodbye to all their newly made friends.

Fortunately for the siblings, they would be coming back to Nikas during the next school holiday. But some other godlings, like Alexa and Leon, would be staying behind to get tutored by Mr Lewis, head of human teachings and basic human skills.

The five had all promised each other that they would never get themselves in anything like this again. Their first quest looked like it could've been their last. They were all too young to die.

Jack and Lily were honestly going to miss the others. In fact, Lily was so emotional that, on purpose, she had left her headphones behind so that she could get one last goodbye.

'How's it been without your mum and me?'

'Terrible,' Jack replied. 'I'm just glad that we're all together as a family now.'

'I know,' Tamara said. 'After ten years, we're finally back together, and your dad and I are never, ever going to leave you behind again.'

The Stone family walked into the distance.

'Turn the TV off. And you guys know I don't like you watching stuff like that before bed.'

'Whatever, Mum. It's not like it's real or anything.'

Tamara had told the kids to get tucked up in bed, and the children, who were in no mood for an argument, did exactly that.

As Lily went up towards the staircase of the new Stone house, Jack began to scan the room for a book to read.

"You coming?"

Jack turned, "Yeah, just a sec."

His eyes caught a sudden glimpse of the spine of *Harry Potter and the Half-Blood Prince*, and just as Jack went to pick up the paperback which he had decided he would read for the rest of the week, he thought back to the quest he had been on only days before. Jack knew they had done extremely well, but more than once, he had felt some sort of sixth sense. A feeling he could not describe. Whenever the boy felt it, he could hear it waning him. But what was it warning him of? What was it trying to keep him safe from? Following quests?

Mr and Mrs Stone could feel it as well—something was wrong with their son. He had explained his quest, beginning to end, to them, and they knew that he had succeeded, yet it was as if something was bothering him. Something unknown. Whatever it was, they were not going to let it get in the way of their new life.

Daniel was too old to play football now that he was in his thirties, so instead he had become a banker. They lived only a few minutes from Stamford Bridge, and they had already seen a few matches. And Jack's grades were now better than ever. He had received top grades in almost every subject. Lily's teacher had even called the Stones, commenting on how creative her writing was and on her knowledge of Greek mythology. According to the Stone parents, Jack and Lily were soon to have a little sister. Yet another piece of amazing. So far life was going brilliantly for the Stones.

But, my dear reader, you and I both now that something was wrong. You and I both know that the vicious and cruel journey isn't over for the Stone brother and sister yet. Just not yet. . .

Lightning Source UK Ltd.
Milton Keynes UK
UKOW02f0159220416

272717UK00001B/61/P